the GREAT RACE

The Story of the Chinese Zodiac

Written by **Dawn** Casey

Illustrated by **Anne** Wilson

Barefoot Books
Celebrating Art and Story

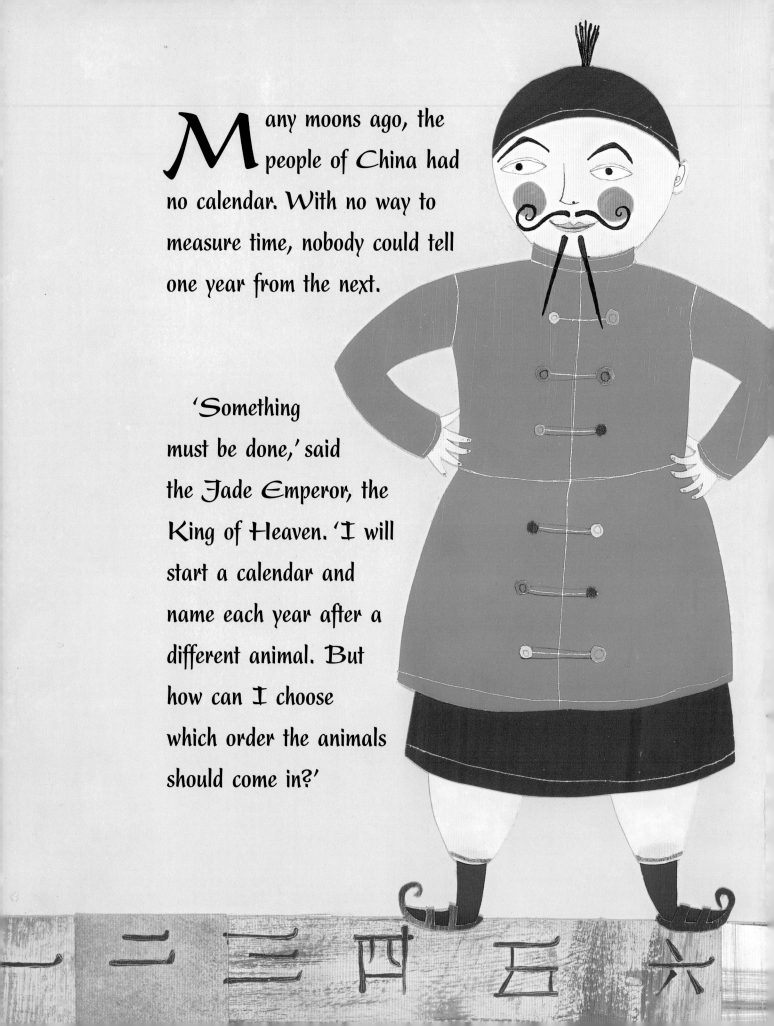

Many moons ago, the people of China had no calendar. With no way to measure time, nobody could tell one year from the next.

'Something must be done,' said the Jade Emperor, the King of Heaven. 'I will start a calendar and name each year after a different animal. But how can I choose which order the animals should come in?'

'I'll hold a race!' the Jade Emperor decided.
'Yes — a swimming race across a wide river! I
will name the years in the order that the animals
finish. The first year of our new calendar shall
be named after the winner!'
He invited every creature in the
kingdom to compete.

Back then, Rat and Cat were best of
friends. They travelled to the river together in
great excitement.

But when they arrived their spirits dropped.
The river was strong and swift. It rushed past
with a deafening roar.

'And just look at all the other animals!'
wailed Cat.

High above, circling in the
sky, soared a creature with the head
of a camel, the horns of a deer, a
long beard and eyes of fire:
Dragon!

Below him, Tiger prowled back and forth.

Swinging
from tree to tree
was Monkey,
chattering with excitement.

Snake was coiled around a branch.
Rat thought she looked very calm.

Close by, Ox waited patiently.

Pig was wallowing
happily in a pool of mud.

Dog bounded around wagging his tail.

Hare was gazing up at the moon, which was still faintly visible in the sky.

Sheep sat watching Cockerel preen his fine feathers.

And Horse stamped his hooves and shook his glossy mane.

'I am the smallest animal here,' said Rat.
'We'll never win!' howled Cat.

Rat was silent. But his
whiskers flickered and his
tail twitched, and there was a
gleam in his beady eye.
'Wait here,' he told Cat.
     'I've got a
        plan.'

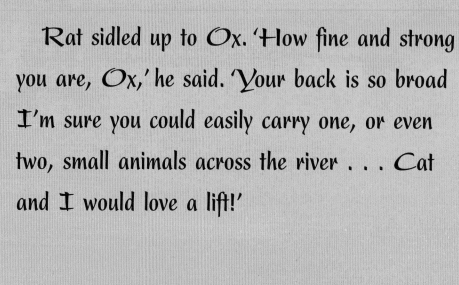

Rat sidled up to Ox. 'How fine and strong you are, Ox,' he said. 'Your back is so broad I'm sure you could easily carry one, or even two, small animals across the river . . . Cat and I would love a lift!'

'Of course, dear Rat,' Ox replied. 'You can depend on me.'

And so Rat and Cat climbed onto Ox's back.

The Jade Emperor shouted,
'Ready . . .
Steady . . .

. . . GO!'

There was a great squawking and bleating and snorting as the animals plunged into the water.

Ox swam sure and steady. It was such a smooth ride that Cat curled up between Ox's shoulders. He closed his eyes and began to purr.

Rat could see Pig still
relaxing near the shore.
And soon they passed Dog, who was
playing in the water.

'Come on, Ox!'
urged Rat.

Meanwhile, Cockerel had spotted something.
'A raft!' he crowed triumphantly. 'Come on up,'
he called to Monkey and Sheep.

'This looks fun!' Monkey shrieked as he
sprang aboard.

'But are you sure it's safe?' Sheep asked,
clambering up.

Rat watched the raft wobbling as Ox
swam past.

Overhead, Dragon curled through the clouds. He was too big to swim in the river so the Emperor had told him to race through the sky, braving the winds instead.

'We're getting closer, Ox,' shouted Rat. 'Keep going!'

Ox swam on, sure and steady.

Now they were catching up
with Hare.

Hare had sat gazing at the silvery
moon for a long time, and it had given her
an idea. She was hopping from round grey
stone to round grey stone across the river.

And there was Tiger, using all his
strength to battle through the currents.

Ox swam on, sure and steady. 'Now we're in the lead!' cried Rat. Rat could just see the Jade Emperor, waiting on the shore.

He looked down at Cat, still snoozing in the sun. 'Lazy animal!' he thought to himself. 'He'll have all his energy left when we arrive. He'll be able to run fast and he'll get to the finish line before me!'

Quick as a wink, Rat saw his chance. He sneaked up close behind Cat and . . .

Ox turned to see what had made the splash. He couldn't see Cat. But he could see the other animals — and they were getting closer. He swam onwards.

Just as Ox was about to step onto dry land . . .

. . . down leapt Rat and darted into first place.

'The winner!' the Jade Emperor declared. 'The first year will be named after Rat.'

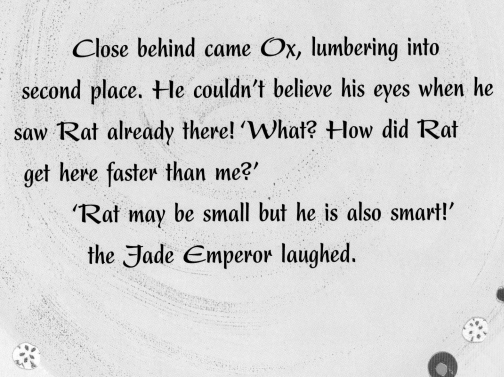

Close behind came Ox, lumbering into second place. He couldn't believe his eyes when he saw Rat already there! 'What? How did Rat get here faster than me?'

'Rat may be small but he is also smart!' the Jade Emperor laughed.

Soon after, Tiger streaked past. 'Third!' called the Jade Emperor.

Next came Hare. Then Dragon swooped out of the sky into fifth place.

Horse was just about to climb onto dry land when from between his feet out slithered Snake.

''Ssscuse me, horsssse,' said Snake, as she slid into sixth place. Horse thundered by seventh.

Sheep was eighth, Monkey ninth and Cockerel tenth. Dog came eleventh and then Pig.

'I needed to stop for a snack,' Pig explained.

'Pig is the twelfth and last animal in the calendar,' the Jade Emperor declared. 'Well done, everyone! You each used your own special skills to cross the river. From now on, every child born in your year will share your talents.'

But what about Cat?

Cat was still splashing and spluttering in the river. He was trying to swim but he hated the water — he just couldn't make it to the shore.

That is why there is no Year of the Cat in the Chinese calendar. And why, to this very day, Cat and Rat are still the worst of enemies.

'Never mind,' said the Jade Emperor as he fished the dripping Cat out of the river. 'You tried your best and that's what's important. Now, let's celebrate!'

And the Jade Emperor
rewarded all the animals with a
wonderful party. There was dancing
and decoration, feasting and
firecrackers, and the animals rejoiced
and wished each other wealth,
health and happiness.

The Chinese Calendar

The Chinese calendar is quite different from the Western calendar. It is based on the movements of the moon. Each month is measured by the way the moon appears to grow bigger and smaller. One month measures one whole cycle of the moon.

As in the Western calendar, there are twelve months in the year, but there are also twelve years in the Chinese calendar cycle. Each year is named after a different animal and each animal comes around in turn, once every twelve years.

Several different stories explain how the twelve animals were chosen for the calendar. The ancient legend you have just read tells how their order was decided by a great race.

Important Days in the Chinese Calendar

Chinese New Year

New Year is the most important festival for Chinese people all around the world. According to the Chinese calendar, the New Year begins with the new moon. This happens on a different date each year, but is usually sometime in late January or early February. That is why the New Year is also known as the Spring Festival.

People prepare for it by cleaning their houses, cooking special foods, buying new clothes and making banners decorated with good luck wishes. Then the festivities begin! There are dragon dances and lion dances, lanterns and firecrackers and wonderful feasts to celebrate the new beginning.

Dragon Boat Festival

The Dragon Boat Festival is held in the middle of summer. It began as a way of trying to please Dragon, who lived in the river and controlled the rains. Nowadays people remember the life of Qu Yuan, a famous poet who lived over two thousand years ago. The festival is celebrated with Dragon Boat races. People race long rowing boats carved and painted to look like fierce dragons.

Moon Festival

This is a harvest festival. It is held in the middle of autumn when the moon is full and bright. As the sun sets, children parade through the streets carrying candlelit lanterns. People gather together in the cool night air to gaze at the moon. The Chinese think that the marks on the moon look like a hare — they tell stories explaining how Hare came to live on the moon. Everybody enjoys eating moon-cakes — round pastries with a sweet filling.

The Characters of the Twelve Animals

Each of the twelve animals in the Chinese calendar has a different character. The Chinese believe that your own character depends on which animal was ruling in the year you were born. They say: 'This is the animal that hides in your heart.'

Find the year you were born in and discover your own animal sign:

Rat:
1936, 1948, 1960, 1972, 1984, 1996, 2008
Rats are clever, ambitious and quick-witted. They get on well with Dragons and Monkeys.

Hare:
1939, 1951, 1963, 1975, 1987, 1999, 2011
Hares are lucky, kind and peaceful. They get on well with Sheep and Pigs.

Ox:
1937, 1949, 1961, 1973, 1985, 1997, 2009
Oxen are honest, patient and hard-working. They get on well with Snakes and Cocks.

Dragon:
1940, 1952, 1964, 1976, 1988, 2000, 2012
Dragons are powerful, strong and energetic. They get on well with Rats and Monkeys.

Tiger:
1938, 1950, 1962, 1974, 1986, 1998, 2010
Tigers are brave, powerful and daring. They get on well with Horses and Dogs.

Snake:
1941, 1953, 1965, 1977, 1989, 2001, 2013
Snakes are calm, wise and elegant. They get on well with Oxen and Cocks.

Horse:

1942, 1954, 1966, 1978, 1990, 2002, 2014

Horses are popular, independent and fun. They get on well with Tigers and Dogs.

Cockerel:

1945, 1957, 1969, 1981, 1993, 2005, 2017

Cockerels are adventurous, kind and hard-working. They get on well with Snakes and Oxen.

Sheep:

1943, 1955, 1967, 1979, 1991, 2003, 2015

Sheep are artistic, loving and tender-hearted. They get on well with Hares and Pigs.

Dog:

1946, 1958, 1970, 1982, 1994, 2006, 2018

Dogs are loyal, affectionate and generous. They get on well with Tigers and Horses.

Monkey:

1944, 1956, 1968, 1980, 1992, 2004, 2016

Monkeys are happy, confident and enthusiastic. They get on well with Dragons and Rats.

Pig:

1947, 1959, 1971, 1983, 1995, 2007, 2019

Pigs are noble, helpful and forgiving. They get on well with Hares and Sheep.

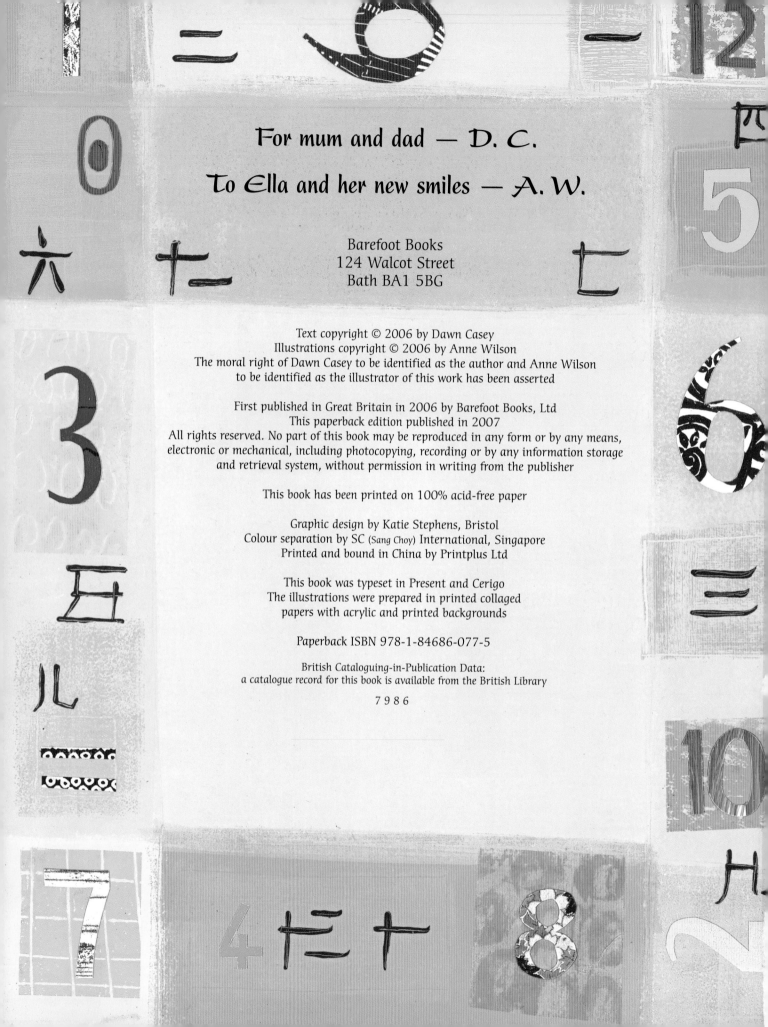

For mum and dad — D. C.

To Ella and her new smiles — A. W.

Barefoot Books
124 Walcot Street
Bath BA1 5BG

Text copyright © 2006 by Dawn Casey
Illustrations copyright © 2006 by Anne Wilson
The moral right of Dawn Casey to be identified as the author and Anne Wilson
to be identified as the illustrator of this work has been asserted

First published in Great Britain in 2006 by Barefoot Books, Ltd
This paperback edition published in 2007

This book has been printed on 100% acid-free paper

Graphic design by Katie Stephens, Bristol
Colour separation by SC (Sang Choy) International, Singapore
Printed and bound in China by Printplus Ltd

This book was typeset in Present and Cerigo
The illustrations were prepared in printed collaged
papers with acrylic and printed backgrounds

Paperback ISBN 978-1-84686-077-5

British Cataloguing-in-Publication Data:
a catalogue record for this book is available from the British Library

7 9 8 6